Herbert Bates

Songs of Exile

Herbert Bates

Songs of Exile

ISBN/EAN: 9783337181468

Printed in Europe, USA, Canada, Australia, Japan

Cover: Foto ©Andreas Hilbeck / pixelio.de

More available books at **www.hansebooks.com**

SONGS OF EXILE
BY HERBERT BATES

SICVT LILIVM

INTER SPINAS

BOSTON COPELAND AND DAY
M D CCC XCVI

CONTENTS

CONTENTS

SONGS OF EXILE

FROM sea and plain, from prairie sprent
   With riotous sunflowers indolent,
From billows flashing bloom of spray,
From many an alien place they stray —
These rhymes.   No arduous flight their
    song, —
Awed honor to earth's swift and strong
And sweet.   Night's vast, the dreamy
    boon
Of odorous noon,
Dread instancy of Death, the might of
    love, —
All rapture, all above
That lifts, enchants, appeals, — music that
    bears
The key of tears, —
Worship and awe and wonder, — these
    have stirred
This answering word.
And these to thee I bring,
Who brought me spring, —
Dearest and wife.   Be all that love has
    done,
    Love's dower alone.

EXILES OF PLAIN

A DISROOTED FIR—TREE IN A PRAIRIE TOWN

HOW didst thou ever come
So far from thy heaped rocky home,
Tree of the hills and sea ?
What fate's divorcement, what abrupt exile,
Severed thy stem and led thee here, like me,
By many an obstinate mile
Shut from the dear, barred bliss of all that
  used to be.
Thy light wind-poising sprays
Perhaps in summer days
Hung o'er some tide-gorged cove,
By cool, remote, reef-barred Atlantic bays,
Fog-gated, mountain-walled,
Where red-beaked gulls would rove
In clamorous flocks, and sleep
Like bubbled foam-heaps on the glassy deep,
When all the winds were still.

And there thou stoodst, and sea-caves under
  thee, —
The pebbled, shell-strewn caverns of the sea,
Where curious fish came nosing, rolling slow

2

In the cold clear swaying swell, —
And overhead thou feltst the breezes blow :
The hard north wind, that sharpened like
    miracle
The distant shores, and drew
From far-off isles the blue
Dreamed veil of distance, till, o'er miles of
    sea,
Thy brethren answered thee
From where they stood on some sea-breast-
    ing promontory ;
The keen north wind, glad-eyed,
Song-hearted, triumph-strong,
With flawless blue of pale sky pitiless
And tingling life, who caught from thy
    stirred tress
Sweet scent, balsamic, like,
Alas, the odorous summonings that strike
My senses as I bend above thee here,
And bid the dead past near !
Like seaweed, tinged with sea,
Gathered and sent memorial to me,
Which, when I placed it in clean water,
    gave,
Even to that pale water of the plain,
Waif of some thunderous rain,

The harsh, sweet scent of the Atlantic wave,
Stinging my eyes to saltness with this scent
So richly redolent
Of all the empurpled wealth of clouded
  main,
Drawing me back again
To walk the pebbled, ocean-beaten floor,
And hear the backward roar
Of the resorbent anger of the deep.
So thy scent wakes from sleep
Old days of north wind, when I giddily
Clambered the bastions high
Of eastern crags, and pierced the caverned
  ways
That filing sheep had tracked,
Burrowing, woolly-backed,
To reach some vantage-point of cliff, and
  see,
Beneath, the green foam spreading thunder-
  ously ;
And, following in their track,
I stood alone, on some cleft pinnacle,
And saw the sombre swell
Heave shoreward under all the rippled ranks,
To beat against the rocky barrier-banks
That set God's limit to the world-wide sea.

EXILES OF PLAIN

All this thou bringst to me ;
And then the picture changes, and the south
(Not there the wind of drouth)
Drives from his tented camp
His fog-hosts of the damp,
To shut into the silence of the hoar
And century-hearted sea
The youth and green redundance of the
  shore.

Once more, tumultuously,
I hear the trumpets of the east wind blow
The onset of the embattled air,
The summons of the gale ;
And watch the gray-heaved sea, sprent
  fiercely pale,
With spouting spume of wrath,
And the wind's serpent path,
Foam-written, undulous along the waves,
And hear the choking caves,
The barking, surly cannon of the deep.
Along the seaward steep,
Besieging billows shoot their foamy towers ;
Eastward, the ranged scud lowers ;
And, seaward far, I catch
Glimpses of staggering ships that match
Their power with the plumèd ranks of sea

And this, — discountried tree, —
All this has once been thine
As it has once been mine —
Thine, whose sweet scent to me
Is mixed memorially
With the keen savor of the wind-rent brine.

Tree of the rocky nest, of pinnacles
Where only the bird dwells,
Nor smoke of men, nor fields bestreaked
    with plows,
Nor care-bewrinkled brows
Come ever to intrude
Upon thy stern, stone-rooted solitude ;
Alas ! that thou shouldst stand
An exile in a stoneless land,
Where never hill may raise
Its sudden skyward summit in God's praise ;
Where the sleek hill-slopes swerve
In russet, serpent curve
To the dark draws where tawniest sunflowers
    nod,
And sun-seared golden-rod ;
Where league-wide fields of pallid grain,
    dusk-furrowed
And gopher-burrowed,
Roll dizzy to the borders of the sight,

EXILES OF PLAIN

A dim vast land of level light,
Pallid and vacuous,
Windily tenuous,
Swept with the dusty south,
Parched with the summer drouth,
Fair with its fairness, but in that is none
That thou canst call thine own.

For love comes not of wish or will,
But clings unalterable
To the old dear sights that first
Filled the child's eyes, and nursed
His thoughts to song. What new-seen sights
  of mine
Can speak the message of the wind-crowned
  pine
That, solitary, crowned my hill of home !
What voice shall ever come
From rippled corn speechful as came that
  slow
Surged speech, as to and fro
It swayed to murmurous cadence of the
  wind !
What mystery shall I find
In plains explorable to match with thee,
Stern, man-denying sea,
With wide, fog-vistaed ways untraceable

By furrow of any steel !
What speech have sulky sunflowers that star
The prairie ridge afar
To match the message childhood's daisy
    gave,
Or the flame-glad field-lily, or such sea-
    bloom
As wavered in the ocean cave
Through shattered emerald gloom !

    I have no skill of these,
My spirit is the sea's,
The rocky land's, — aspiring hardier ways
To greet the blaze
Of bluer, tenderer skies
Wilful with tears, grief-tremulous, like the
    eyes
That are indeed love's own.

    For Nature's level tone,
Eternal smile, perpetual placitude,
I love not, turning, rather, in my heart
To such friend as thou art,
O stern Atlantic sea,
Misted with petulance of hovering storm,
Snow-blurred, — or summer-warm, —
Idle and amorous with transient kindliness ;

Thy changeful tress
Now tossed with tenderest breeze, now ser-
     pent-spread
The tempest's Gorgon halo of thy head,
Medusa-terrible, —
Thy voice, now keening with the hate of hell,
Now fluting heaven's tropic, gold-bright
     halls, —
Now, with fierce trumpet-calls,
Shaking the heart of the lighthouse sentinel,
Jarring the granite walls
That barrier thy wrath, tolling the knell
Of thy slain sons on many a wave-poised
     buoy, —
Now soothing, with the joy
Of starriest dream, the muffled roll of peace
Sung by phosphoric seas
That tramp the sodden sulkiness of sand
Along the grumbling land.

How oft with swaying keel
Have I dared forth to feel
The gliding long relapses of thy wave ;
How oft from cave to cave
Have wandered the bored bastions of the
     coast,
And scared the piping host

Of ghostly gulls that dreamed above my
    ways, —
Have entered silent bays
Where the smooth swell broke bubbling up
    the beach,
Learned all thy lore could teach
Of veering fish, of ridgy porpoises,
And all the tinier beauties of thine home,
Dense seaweed, where the foam
Lay balled in tremulous wreath,
And felt thy invigorate breath
From sparkling sundering depths of emerald
Flecked with green-hearted gold —
The mottled splendor of the prisoned sun.

And now those days are done.
Only this wide plain witnesses the sea,
Only the lone infinity
That hungers to no end,
A land that seems not as a friend,
A russet, stirless plain, whose lucent skies
Like bold unfaltering eyes
Burn steadfast all the hours of summer
    through.

So I as you,
Tree-friend, sea-sundered friend,

EXILES OF PLAIN

Disrooted, ponder ; and, compassionate,
Muse thine uprooted fate,
And pray thy pity, even as mine for thee.
God grant that we may see
Some day the old ranged cliffs of home
  again ;
But, if it be not, — vain
If hope and prayer be, — still
Old memories shall thrill
Our dreams in darkness, and these sights
  shall stand
Beyond life's bounds to greet,
In the dazed dawning of some ultimate land,
Our wandered feet.

In heaven there is no sea ?
Then heaven is none for me,
Far rather would I rove
The old earth-places that I used to love,
And with the sea-bird's flight
Swoop up the wave's green imminence of
  light,
And skim the caverned wall
Of ocean cliffs where the majestical
And sullen headlands gloom the icy seas,
Or drift in spacy ease
Of ocean boundlessness,

Till Time, with stress
Of his frore hand, shall chill the shrinking
   sun,
And day be done,
And cold congeal the caverns of the sea.
Then let my slumber be
Swift, dearest Death, or lead me on, afar,
To some out-spherèd star,
To some new planet where
New hills rise fair,
Where the long breakers melt along the
   misted bar,
And the sea's ancient scent breathes up the
   spacious air.

A SONG OF THE DROUTH

HIS slow mules plodded on,
   And he heard the worn wheels clack,
And the voice of the thin, sad wind
    As it whined behind his back.

For the wind cried out of the south,
    The wind of the heat and dust,
The gray wind of the drouth,
    That says, " Thou must ! "

A SONG OF THE DROUTH

Thou must arise and go,
Whether thou wilt or no,
For the land throbs parched to death,
And the shrivelled maize sobs dead,
And the burnt wheat bows the head,
And the gray dust stifles breath.
Whether thou wilt or no,
Thou must arise and go.
Thy sod-built house that stands
The heaped work of thine hands,
The fields thy beasts have ploughed,
The crops thine hands have sowed,
The hopes thy heart has builded,
The future, vision-gilded,
The room where thy child breathed life,
The grave where sleeps thy wife, —
Whether thou wilt or no,
Thou must leave them all, must go.

Over the beaten track,
With the thin wind at thy back,
Plodding the powdered dust
That climbs to the swirling gust, —
Where the hungry coyote cries,
Where the outcast farm-beast dies,
Through the seared, crisp hiss of corn,
Under brown trees, burnt, forlorn,

13

Past the houses, empty, bare
Of hope, to the old home where
Life promised, long ago,   .   .   .
The fulfilment to-day you know.

Ah, what are the old home places,
If they frame not the old home faces?
What glint upon boyhood's stream,
When dead is the boyhood dream?
What charm can linger still
To the firs on the ridging hill
If you clasp no more her hand
There where you used to stand ;
If far away she lies
With the plains-dust in her eyes,
Alone, in the dusty dearth
Of the clodded, iron earth?
Is it her voice that sighs
Behind in the wind that cries,
Her voice that bids you stay,
Die where she died, not stray
Back to the old east home,   ˋ
Where she may never come?

Back to the hopeless home,
      Back, with the sobbing wind
Lamenting in thine ears,
      Back, with thy life behind,

CHARTER-DAY POEM

Through the hissing, sun-seared fields,
    Through the drift of the sullen dust,
At the gray will of the drouth,
    That says, "Thou must!"

CHARTER-DAY POEM, UNIVER-
SITY OF NEBRASKA

THE hunter shook from his brown pipe
    the spark
That flashed into the dark
Of the knotted grass-roots, and grew strong
    and sprang
Into crackling flame, and it heard the wind
    that sang
Its dry keen wail o'er the prairies, and
    strengthened and grew
Till it flared to a league-long flame, and
    the scared birds flew,
Smoke-blinded before it, and the blundering
    buffalo fled,
And the coyote quacked in his covert, and
    the Indian said :
"To-night the God of the fire has raised his
    head !"

From the fire of ancient worlds a little spark,
    chance-shaken,
Fell on our alien plains, and spread alone,
And strengthened till it shone
World-wide ; and nations said: When did it
    waken ?
We saw not its birth, but to-day we see,
    afar,
A flame that darkens the low sunset star,
And drives the huddled night
Cowering before the lances of its light.

For a voice cried in the ear
Of the West: Awake, for the future calls
    thee ! Hear,
Child of the plain, to-day your limbs are
    strong,
Your eyes are radiant ! Wake, for you sleep
    too long !
Wake, for the east hills quicken into day,
And the gray wind of morning calls to
    song !
Wake, for within your heart there glows
    The prompting of the new-born soul,
Strenuous and tireless, quickening as it
    knows,
    Far off, the destined goal !

CHARTER-DAY POEM

The golden sunflowers, myriad-blossoming,
    blaze
  From hill to golden hill;
And melt at last into the golden haze
  Of the great distance.   All the land is still
With solitude, and only the quick bird
Chirps in the grass ; no other sound is heard
To praise God's golden gift.
The white clouds sail and sift
The mottled moonlight over the wide land,
The slow streams flow ; the narrow forests
    stand
Huddled and timorous for loneliness.
Has God not given gifts enough to bless
Our singers from their silence ?   Has our ear
Grown all too dull to hear
The still, sweet voice of Nature's tenderness ?
Has she no whisper to awake
The soul that dreams, the song that sleeps,
Until its thrilling chords shall shake
  To the gray hearts of older lands,
To where the ocean's iron deeps
  Complain upon their endless sands ?

To love, to know, to sing, — these three
  Are God's most precious gifts to men,

To know what has been, and to see
The ripening of what shall be,
  Far off beyond the present's ken.
To read life's book, and understand ;
    To tell the treasury of stars,
    And through Death's unrelenting bars
To spy the bounds of spirit-land.

  To love, to know life fair, to see
Earth beautiful, till each gray tree
Shall tell its message, each star shine
Some consolation, and the line
Of the last hills shall speak of peace ;
Till war and hate and envy cease,
And over all the smiling land shall chime
The petalled joy-bells of God's blossom-
    time.

  To sing, to tell it all,
As the glad birds that call
The green spring up the land, till each
With happier heart shall learn and teach
Such new accord of life as sings attune
Through the dense leaves of June.

  To know, to love, to sing, — and then,
To spread the gathered wealth abroad

CHARTER-DAY POEM

To every dwelling-place of men,
As, with the ancient dragon-hoard,
Siegfried, the slayer, southward rode
With the red serpent gold that glowed,
All glorious, at his saddle-bow.

Ride on, O conqueror, with thy spoil
    Of error and thy gifts of might !
Ride on, that every heart may know
    The sudden sun of wisdom's light,
That through the loneliest prairie ways,
    Where the least sod-built shanty stands,
    Or where the city's million hands
Toil grimy through the grudging days,
The blessing of thy gifts may go,
That our new land may rise and know,
As the old peoples of the past,
The joys that do not pale, the hopes that
        last
Against the hour of death, and make of life
More than a barren strife,
And of life's end no mere forgetfulness.
So shall thy mission be to bless,
To raise, to brighten, and to lead us on
Till the last fight is won,
The utmost end accomplished, and we see
Far up above us, white and marvellous,

The peaks long-sought, and hear acclaim-
    ing us
The voices of old victors gloriously
Triumphing up the slopes of victory.

HOME

INTO the East and away from the plain,
    In the west wind's track we roam ;
Over the waving wastes of grain,
Till we come to the heaped, stern hills again,
    Till we come to the hills of home.

The pine trees nod on the windy crest,
    The clean streams flash below,
And oh, for the calm, firm, rocky rest,
The stubborn strength of the earth's ribbed
        breast,
    And the flowers our old eyes know !

We have delved the black of the prairie earth,
    The muck of the rotting sod,
We have shared the drouth and the rain-rot
        dearth,
We have sorrowed, have laughed with the
        devil's mirth,
    In a land that knew no God.

HOME

We have coined black mould into gleaming
    gold,
  We have minted the green of grain,
The strength of our lives is spent and sold —
And now we are old, and the tale is told,
  And God knows whose the gain !

Here's off with the slime of the clinging clay,
  And the stench of the dense sunflowers,
And the dry keen wind that cries all day —
And away, oh my heart, away and away,
  To the old loved land of ours !

To our own loved land, where the white
    gull swoops,
  Where the salted sea-wind cries,
Where the taut sheet drips, and the lee rail
    scoops,
And the gray, long veil of the rain-squall
    stoops
  From the wrack of the scudding skies.

Into the East, from the dread of the plain,
  In the west wind's track we come.
God bring us safe through the wastes of grain,
Safe back to the heaped sea-hills again,
  Safe back to the hills of home.

PRAIRIE

ACROSS the sombre prairie sea
The dark swells billow heavily.
Are the looming ridges near or far
That heave to the smooth horizon-bar?

The russet reach of grassy roll
Sickens the heart and numbs the soul,
The thin wind gives no air for breath,
The stillness is the pause of death.

This width was never shaped to be
The home of man's mortality,
A breathless vacuum of peace,
Where life's spent ripples spread and cease.

No end, no source, its spaces know,
Wide as the sea's perpetual flow
Is its dead stand — dull wall on wall
Of sullen waves unspiritual.

God give me but in dream to come
Back to the pine-clad hills of home,
Back to the old eternity
Of placid, all-consoling sea.

COLD

THE last sunflower stalk is burnt,
  The last of the bread is gone,
And cold across the snow-swept plain
  Comes gray the aching dawn.

The thin grass rustles by the door,
  The windows jar and cry,
The white drift sifts through the broken pane,
  And the ceaseless snow throngs by.

Hush — sleep, my little one ; soon enough
  The long sleep soothes thy pain —
Ah, I could sleep, for the dull cold
  Burns into my brain !

The shuddering coyote whines and cries,
  And howls to God for food ;
The great gray wolves troop down arow
  And pause and sniff for blood.

O God, who feed'st the whining beast,
  Send meat to those that pray ;
Thou, God, that giv'st the bird his feast,
  Be thou our help to-day !

23

In the breathless cruel cold, give help,
  And bring the spring again,
And ridge the long hills with the great
  Green heritage of grain.

ON THE PRAIRIE

BARE, low, tawny hills
  With bluer heights beyond,
And the air is sweet with spring,
  But when will the earth respond?

Prairie that rolls for leagues,
  Dusky and golden-pale,
Like a stirless sea of waves,
  Unbroken by ship or sail.

The hollows are dark with brush,
  And black with the wash of showers,
And ragged with bleaching wreck
  Of the ranks of the tall sunflowers.

No cloud in the blue, no stir
  Save the shrill of the wind in the grass,
And the meadow-lark's note, and the call
  Of the wind-borne crows that pass.

THE PIONEERS

Bare, low, tawny hills,
  With bluer heights beyond,
And the air is sweet with spring,
  But when will the earth respond?

THE PIONEERS

PALE in the east a filmy moon
  Creeps up the empty sky,
And the pallid prairie rounds bleak below,
  And we wonder that we are here ; and the
    thin winds sigh
  Through the broken stalks of the sun-
    flowers that wait to die,
And the sun is gone, and the darkness be-
  gins to grow,
  And out on the shadowy plains we hear
    the coyote's cry.

Out of the dark of the prairie plains —
What lurks in the darkened plains?
  It is there that the coyote howls,
  It is there that the Indian prowls,
Sinewy-footed, alert,
Watching to do us hurt ;
  And the sombre buffalo
  Pace, ominous and slow,

With their black beards trailing low
Over the sifting snow.
    And we, we cower and shake,
    Lying all night awake, —
We in our little sod-built hut in the heart of
    the plain.

God guard us, and make vain
    The wiles of the Indian foe ;
    God show us how to go,
And lead us in again
Out of the dread of the plain,
    Home to the mountains and hills that our
    childhood knew,
    Where over the sombre pine-trees the sea
    shines blue.

SPRING ON THE PRAIRIE

OVER the stubborn earth,
Over the sullen fields,
Spring bent her brooding wings
Of sombre thunder-cloud,
Whispering: "Wake from dearth ;
Wake, and your answer yield !"
And the low clouds bent and bowed,
And the thunder muttered loud,

SPRING ON THE PRAIRIE

And the driving raindrops fell,
And the hail, and earth answered well.
The little grass that slept,
In tiny headlets crept
Up to the warmth and air.
And the trees, black-boughed and bare,
Drank a new life that flushed
To their tender tips, and blushed
In the ribbed soft youth of leaves.
And the warm earth flowered in scent
Bounteous, indolent,
All the black wealth of plain
Answering the pulsing rain.
And the meadow-lark called his keen
Flute-note of joy between.
Across the new-sown rows
Cawed the slow, lumbering crows,
Jag-winged and greedy-eyed.
And all that it seemed had died,
All that had cowered dumb,
Awoke and stirred and cried,
For over the prairies wide
The spirit of spring had come.

FAR AWAY

FAR away, in seaward places
  The bristled fir-trees nod,
And the bluebells lift their faces,
  And the pine holds hands to God.

The low sea moans and grumbles
  Upon the rounded stones,
And the clean white foam-line tumbles,
  And the wind of ocean moans.

And the slant-winged sea-gull, gleaming
  Over the sea-blue bay,
Seems mine own soul — who dreaming,
  Sit westward, far away.

THE GIANT WOLF

THE giant wolf, the woodland wolf,
  Strode southward down the wind,
And the gale yelled keen, and the moon
    gleamed green,
  And the little stars blinked blind.

PEISINOË

The seething snow-snakes twined before,
  And hissed through the knotted grass,
And he heard overhead the sheeted dead,
  That dance in the whirlwind, pass.

His shag gray locks roughed with the wind,
  His white teeth fanged with wrath ;
Now God be good to the man whose blood
  He smells before his path !

Now God be good to the man whose feet
  On the snow-blind, swirling way,
Shall meet the blaze of his hungry gaze
  And the snarling fangs that slay.

And happy he that sits at home,
  Where the corn-fire smoulders warm,
When alone, in the white of the whirling
    night,
  The gray wolf walks the storm.

PEISINOË

THE old, old song of the old sea,
  The ancient sea, the serpent sea,
A lady fair, with gleaming eyes,
Beneath a gnarlèd tree.

29

A lady fair with gleaming eyes,
With golden hair, coiled serpentwise
   Round slender throat, round white limbs
     bare
To strange and sunset skies.

My wealth, my weal, O lady fair,
My serpent queen, my lady fair,
   Land, life, for one kiss of thy mouth
Amid thy golden hair !

Her stretched arms call : He follows fleet.
Her sudden kiss burns sharp and sweet,
   His eyes are blind ; he may not see
The pit beneath her feet.

The old, old song of the old sea,
The ancient sea, the serpent sea,
   A lady fair, with gleaming eyes,
Beneath a gnarlèd tree.

THE WINTER SEA

THE sea is stern ; her sternness is
   The anger of the infinite ;
In all her power there is no peace,

AT REST

Her waves' complaint shall never cease
    To sob into the stars' great night.

For the sea knows the whole great girth
    And the circle of the barren sky,
And the small circuit of the earth.
She knows that God is not, that birth
    Leads to the grave where all must lie.

White skeletons of many men
    Gleam in the twilight of her caves;
All these had hope; their trusting ken
Saw God's hand strong to help, but when
    Was God's hand stronger than the
    waves?

Cold cannot bind her with his chains,
    The winter tempest is her breath,
Alone of all things she remains
Pitiless, changeless, — fed with rains
    And harvestings of human death.

AT REST

AT the narrow gate of the wind-swept
    strait,
    The white light towers high,

And black and silent at its foot
    The crippled schooners lie.

With cordless masts and broken decks,
    And sides flush with the sea,
They sleep in the summer sun and dream
    Of the days when they were free.

Like the wild white birds that sought the
    light
    Out of the storm's dark breath,
They swept, wind-winged, through the
    · whirling night,
    And at its foot found death.

WITHIN THE GATES

THE low clouds darken down the hills
    And bar the narrow straits,
Without, the angry ridging sea
    Beats, growling, at the gates.

Without, the gray great sea heaves free,
    The foamy east-wind calls,
And the fir-trees wrestle stubborn boughs
    Along the wave-jarred walls.

THE COMING OF THE STORM

Within, the schooners swing and sway
  By the black, rain-sodden pier,
The swift squalls darken up the bay,
  And the ripples race with fear.

But far outside, in the fog and rain,
  The great ships lift and reel,
And the gray waves roar to pluming flame,
  And the keening sea-birds wheel.

THE COMING OF THE STORM

WHAT darkens in the west?
  (Hark how the gulls are calling!)
The spread black hand of the storm
  That grows with the twilight's falling.

What gathers in the east?
  (Hark how the beaches rattle!)
The march of the columned clouds
  That gather to the battle.

Dark and slow, row on row,
  The ranks of the east assemble,
And under their line the sea's ranks shine,
  And the long shores quake and tremble.

The swift scud streams, the white foam
    gleams,
  And fierce shall the onset be,
And God be his help that strives to-night
  With the armies of the sea !

Black ridges with white, mad manes,
  Beaches that roar and rattle,
And a wind that ranges the wild sea-line,
  Driving the waves to battle.

SEA–GULLS

WHENCE come the white gulls that
      sail,
That flutter and sink and sail ?
Their red beaks flash and glitter,
Their wide wings droop and trail.

They follow the sea-tide's call,
They troop, at the sea-tide's call,
' Over the wide sea-spaces .
And along the dark sea-wall.

Along the dark sea-steep,
By the black cliffs, bare and steep,
They flutter and fall and scream,
They drift slow-winged in sleep.

IN SPRING

They wander and brighten and gleam,
As the wind-clouds shift and gleam —
Souls of sea-winds that wander
In a sea-encircled dream.

ALAS, THE WEARY WHILE!

ALAS, the weary while to spring !
The weary while, the snows to cling,
Ere north the nest-bound swallows wing,
And wide the rapturous south wind fling
The portals of the sun.

Ah, sweet, the weary while to wait,
Till summoning spring shall burst the gate,
And bring, embowered, irradiate,
The hour — ah, sweet, the while to wait
Till springtime be begun !

IN SPRING

LIFE'S but a spark that flares its flame
And sinks to sullen gray ;
But ah, the flame, and the joy of the flame,
Before it dies away !

The breath of the bloom and the blaze of
    the sun,
  And the emerald boon of May,
And the arms of love and the eyes of love
  And the hour that is for aye !

The spring winds storm the whispering hill,
  A sea of glinted spray,
The night-vales throb with the whip-poor-will,
  The moon brings love's mild day, —
For ah, the flame, and the joy of the flame,
  And the blossoming boon of May,
The arms of love and the eyes of love,
  And the hour that lives for aye !

THE BROOK'S GOOD-NIGHT

DID you not hear the whisper,
  In the hollow by the mill ?
For Nature is talking to the brook
  That prattles beneath the hill :
  " Child, will you not be still ?
Will you not sleep ?   Little one, pretty one,
  look,
    It is warm to-day, but the grim north
    wind will come back ;

THE ELM

He is only skulking to-day,
Treading and trampling the tumbled leaves
 in the wood,
 And his brows are bad and black.
Peace, little one, be good,
Be good and be quiet, sleep in your cradle
 of ice,
 And I will throw
Safe over you my coverlet of snow,
My coverlet, to keep
You sheltered in your sleep,
 To keep you sheltered safe from all keen
 winds that blow.
Sleep, darling, have no fear,
For I am with you, dear ! ''

THE ELM

UPON his huge gray-crusted boughs
 The swarming song-birds sing ;
Above, the cawing crow flaps north
 With fringed and sullen wing.

Beneath his feet the grasses start,
 The heart-leaved violets stir,
The south wind whispers of the spring,
 The strong sun tells of her.

His leaves awake not at their touch,
   He waits the stronger rays,
The sultry and supremer hours
   Of May's embowering days.

Then from his giant boughs shall spread
   The green embracing dome,
The arched strong shelter of God's love
   To roof the forest home.

AMONG THE OAKS

NOT in contentment, side by side,
   With lisp of leafy speech,
Spread the broad boughs ; but wander wide,
And crave and yearn unsatisfied,
   And sorrow and beseech.

Each little twig aches out for aid,
   Each leaf lifts hands of prayer ;
Do they, too, ask for God, afraid
At his great silence, and dismayed,
   Finding no answer there ?

O yearning of the aching earth
   That cannot find its fill !

LONE GOD

The little flowers nod with mirth,
Wind-ruffled, but in doubt and dearth
  The great trees sorrow still.

They know, they know. The blank of space
  Bears heavy. Far away
They hear the silence, but always
Against God's unregarding face
  They watch and plead and pray.

LONE GOD

LONE town, crouched in encroaching
    plain,
  Lone ship, encalmed in shimmering sea,
Lone earth, whose ball spins Night's domain,
  Lone soul, that dwells eternity,
Lone sun, whose courtiered course must wait,
  Kin sun, to match thy course with his,
Lone God, enthroned to consummate
  Climaxing time ! In heaven's bliss
Creep no sad notes to thwart the strong
  Uplift of seraph praise — no shade
Darkening gold heaven, that no sweet song
  Sings love, save thou the singer made ?
Creation's pinnacle yearns lone ;
No kin God knows thy God-need, none !

SONG HOMES ON HILLS

SONG homes on hills ; no placid plains
Can hem its powers ; it disdains
Their unaspiring calm, to dare
More arduous air.

The blown Acropolis caught fire
Of song ; the dull Bœotian lyre,
Stagnated, ceased.   Upon the height,
Alone, flamed light.

Up from the plains !   Up where the hills
Stoop windward, where ridged sunset fills.
The vales with misted gold, where trees
Speak windy peace !

Up where the clouds go, where the birds
Stoop reeling, where the heart to words
Leaps as the bird to song, — the strong
Wild nature-song, —

Bird-sung, wind-pealed, pine-trumpeted,
Star-flashed, the clarion to our dead
Aspirings, bidding them stir, arise,
And dare the skies.

IN SOME SWEET PLACE

Song homes on hills, its power disdains
The sordid plains ; its true domains
Where riotous the wild wind thrills —
Its home, the hills !

IN SOME SWEET PLACE OF
SUNSET

IN some sweet place of sunset, where the
    sun
  Sinks and so passes, and the rounded sea
And vacant skv, still, though the day be
    done,
  Pulse with his pale diminished memory,
So the old lustre of those living days,
    When, one with Nature, in her haunts I
    dwelt,
And sought the hill-tops through the salt
    sea-haze,
    And pierced the unwilling wood, or
    gladly knelt
Beside some virgin spring, all rock-embow-
    ered, —
    All these old lustres in my soul still
    gleam,

And through these barren plains I walk, en-
dowered,
    With   sweet   diminished   radiances of
    dream, —
Pale visions, quick to vanish, could I see
O'er eastern hills mine old land smile to me !

THE HEAVENS ARE OUR RIDDLE

THE heavens are our riddle ; and the sea,
    Forested earth, the grassy rustling plain,
Snows, rains, and thunders.   Yea, and even
    we
    Before   ourselves   stand   ominous.   In
    vain !
The stars still march their way, the sea still
    rolls,
    The   forests   wave,   the   plain   drinks   in
    the sun,
And we stand silent, naked, — with tremu-
    lous souls, —
    Before our unsolved selves.   We pray to
    one
Whose hand should help us.   But we hear
    no voice ;

TRANSIENCY

Skies clear and darken ; the days pale
    and pass,
Nor any bids us weep or bids rejoice.
    Only the wind sobs in the shrivelling
    grass, —
Only the wind, — and we with upward eyes
Expectant of the silence of the skies.

TRANSIENCY.

WOULD that I were more than the old
    wind
And the enduring sea — than the blue sky
That sees the dooms of men ; more than
    this blind
    Bright web of thoughtless life that need not
    die.
To-day I am more. I make its wonder
    mine :
    To-morrow my pulse stills ; the wind may
    blow
Unheard above my grave, the sky may shine,
    The blue sea roll its way — I shall not
    know,
Nor these know of me. Nature pays no
    tears

In tribute to her transient lord. He fades
Out from her radiance, and still the years
   Flush with new green the forest-scented
     glades,
Where not a nodding flower shall pine that
   he,
Friend of all tenderest flowers, has ceased
   to be.

AND LOVE, THEY SAY, SHALL FADE

AND love, they say, shall fade, — like
   summer weed
   At winter's frost shall wither, — and
     thou, again,
That smilest now, shalt know love's piteous
   need,
   And empty arms, and uncompanioned pain.
Thy lips shall cease from kisses, and her face
   That shone for thee shall shine to other eyes,
Or slowly, shred by shred, be shorn of grace,
   And pale from the old beauty thou
     didst prize.
Alas, and shall it be? I think not Life,
   Slow builder of sweet love, shall topple
     down

WHO ARE YE

His gradual temple, or the loving wife
  Grow less beloved than who in maiden gown
First won the wavering heart, or time de-
  clare
The face each morn more dear can grow
  less fair.

WHÓ ARE YE THAT HASTE
AWAY

WHO are ye that haste away,
  With figures bowed, with garments
    gray,
Into the deep of the sunset's sleep?

"We are the griefs of yesterday."

Why, gray griefs, do ye take your flight?
What dawn of wonder, what new-born light,
  Shall seal to-morrow from the hosts of
    sorrow?

"Another has come, of greater might."

Who is he, with power above
Your power that all men perish of?

" One tender, yet tearless, with strong heart
    fearless,
The lord of sorrow, the master, Love ! ''

THE MESSAGE

I MADE a little song one day,
  Not over sad nor over gay,
And every word thereof was full
With praise of one most beautiful.

To her I sang it, while o'erhead
The sunset deepened into red
Behind the hills ; word, song, and verse
With utter love made wholly hers.

And so I put it from my heart ;
I said : " My song, since hers thou art,
Save at her bidding it shall be,
Return thou nevermore to me.''

And as I lie to-day, quite still,
Beside her grave upon the hill,
The little song comes back, so clear,
So sweet, I think she sent it here.

BEFORE THE BATTLE

"TO-NIGHT," they said,
    "When the day is dead,
When we are slain, or the foe is fled, —
    At set of sun,
    When all is done,
When all is lost, or the fight is won, —
    Then we shall sleep
    In Death's dark keep,
Or drink the red wine till the night is deep.
    Ride ! Ride !
    With our wrath to guide,
Into the battle, sword by side !

" To-night," they laughed,
    As they stooped and quaffed
The red, fierce wine from the stirrup cup,
    " To-night, when we come,
    The funeral drum
Shall throb to startle their souls that sup ;
    Or the flags shall stream,
    And the banners gleam,
And our trumpets blow triumph as we ride
    up !
    Ride ! Ride !

SONGS OF EXILE

With our wrath to guide,
Into the battle, sword by side !

" Away and away !
For the morn is gray,
And the sword-blades hunger and stir in the
    sheath,
And above the hills
The red sky fills
With the dawning terror of blood beneath.
The white blades burn
And the keen spears yearn
To harvest the red, ripe field of death.
Ride ! Ride !
With our wrath to guide,
Into the battle, sword by side ! "

GRAND MANAN ISLAND

THERE is no sense of human fellowship
    Where rise these cliffs in sea-girt
    majesty ;
Barren and dark, gray with the mystery
Of ocean-wandering clouds that veer and slip
With the wind's changing will, they stand,
    and dip

Their dark foundations in unfathomed sea.
Here all is stern. Here may no kind
gods be.
The strong tide holds all in his iron grip.

Here are no kindly gods, but rather they
That sat sword-girded on the northland
hills,
Giant of purpose, resolute of might,
Watching calm-browed to that fore-destined
day
When all the iron anger of their wills
Should perish in the twilight of the
night.

BEHIND THE BARRIERS

BEHIND the barriers of the sea,
Beside the quiet pools lie we,
On grassy banks, where grow at will
The meadow-sweet and daffodil.

No tree to break the pale blue sky
Where clouds and wind go speeding by,
Hurled inland, not at peace, as we,
Behind the barriers of the sea.

Like a sea-wave, the great sea-wall
Lifts darkling, and the distant fall
Of waters on its outer verge
Shrills sombre with the spreading surge.

But here at rest on banks of flowers,
Small care of wind or waves is ours.
Beside the quiet pools lie we,
Behind the barriers of the sea.

DA CAPO

THE drift of the blushed apple-blossoms,
    falling, falling ;
Petal and sunflake stealing together to the
    bowers of the grass,
And the thrill of the branch-burrowed
    thrushes, calling, calling ;
And the thought — like pale, sun-killing
    cloud — of the blossoms that pass ;
The bloom to the fruit, and the fruit to dull
    earth, to the ultimate seed ;
To ripen, to shoulder to light, to expand
    into deed,
And — die ! Does the dark conquer light, or
    light dominate dark ?

THINE EYES ARE MIRRORS

Ah, God, if God be, shall our spark
Seed us eternal? — The blossoms are falling,
The thrushes are calling, calling.

THINE EYES ARE MIRRORS OF STRANGE THINGS

THINE eyes are mirrors of strange things
   That thou canst never understand,
The secret and the hidden springs
   Of spirit-land.

Thy heart is lighter than the breast
   Of dawn's glad bird that cleaves the skies
To sunlight — but the world's unrest
   Lies in thine eyes.

The yearning of the years that weep
   For all the bliss that shall not be
Dwells in them — thoughts too sadly deep
   To dwell with thee.

These are the shrine where sits thy soul
   Wise in the silence, being dumb
With knowledge of the dread control
   Of days to come.

Thine eyes are mirrors of strange things
  That thou mayst never understand,
The secret ways, the hidden springs,
  Of spirit-land.

BACCALAUREATE HYMN, HAR-VARD, '90

TO Thee, O Father, we whose way
  Lies yet untrodden and untried,
Through joy, through sorrow, humbly pray,
  Be Thou our help, be Thou our guide.

No skill is ours to walk aright
  The path of life with peril strewn ;
No strength is ours save in Thy might,
  No wisdom but in Thee alone.

Through joyous days, through days that weep,
  We fare, with eyes that look to Thee,
On to the last great change of sleep,
  Beyond which waits the life to be.

So guide us, that, in that last hour,
  The battle o'er, the victory won,
We lay the trophies of Thy power
  Before the brightness of Thy throne.

CLASS–DAY ODE, HARVARD, '90

FAIR Harvard, ere we in our turn pass
    away
From thy portals, our song we upraise,
One note in the song of the world-sundered
    throng
Of thy sons, who are one in thy praise ;
From thy throne by the storm-beaten shores
    of the east
To the western, far shores of the sea,
That thy splendor and fame may endure,
    and thy name
In the mouths of thy sons yet to be.

Through the change of the years wherein
    laughter and tears
Shall be mingled as sunshine and shade,
We shall march with thy grace for our guid-
    ance, thy face
Still before us, by dread undismayed.
As the thunder and song of the sea on the
    long
Sea-ramparts, thy praise shall ascend ;
And to thee, who giv'st might to thy sons,
    in the light
Of thy learning, be fame without end.

A SONG OF FALLEN LEAVES

I SAT in the old garden,
   In the ancient, stone-wrought chair,
And the leaves were whirling and falling,
   And I knew that she was there, —

There in the seat beside me,
   And all was as it should —
The leaves from the shuddering branches
   Dropped slow and red as blood.

And I turned to touch, to call her,
   But, lo, she was not there !
Only the leaves fell slowly
   On the ancient, stone-wrought chair.

Oh, love, love of all hours,
   Of waking or of dream,
Come, for the night sinks dreary,
   And I fear the silent stream.

It winds through the windless hollows,
   And with leaves its pools are strown,
And strange dreads watch beside it,
   And I dare not go alone.

DEATH'S DOOR

For I know by the bridge-head yonder
    The spirit of dead glad days
Stands, with drooped eyes, waiting,
    And my soul knows what he says.

And I know that the black still river
    Is deep as a spirit's pain,
And they that sink within it
    Shall never rise again.

DEATH'S DOOR

A WISCONSIN LEGEND

OVER the ice, over the white plains
    hoar, —
Who are these that creep by night,
In the hour of the white midnight
That dare the league-wide passage of Death's
    Door?

Black-haired, with heron-plumes,
He is the king that looms
The midmost in the dance, —
Is that a mortal glance
That his sudden eye reveals?
See where his comrade steals,

See where the whole host come,
Trooping, still, dark and dumb, —
Stealthy Indian spies,
Over the snow-ridged ice !

Long and long ago, —
So runs the tale of woe, —
Indian and bride
Sank in the ice-black tide,
Sunken, seen no more,
In the darkness of Death's Door.

IN THE SILENCE OF THE SUNSET

IN the silence of the sunset,
   By the quiet river's side,
I walked through the sea-sweet meadows
   At the flooding of the tide.

And up the glassy river
   Came a ripple from the sea,
And a gull veered high above me,
   And my soul grew sad in me.

For I thought, In the northern highlands,
   By the northern ocean's foam,
She sits, somewhere at the sunset,
   Far off in her northland home.

AT EVENING

Of her the sea-waves whisper,
  As they ripple through the grass,
Of her the sea-gulls tell me
  As they flutter and wheel and pass.

And to her my heart turns craving,
  Though far away she be,
Across wide wastes of ocean,
  By the cliffs of the northland sea.

AT EVENING

GOD flushed the sunset through the cup
  Of misted hills and said,
  "Now the day is dead,
Earth dark, let thine eyes look up !"

Toil sleeps, care lulls, now cease
  The tumultuous wheels of day,
  And the sun's last ray
Spreads the purple of night's peace.

The curtained mists above
  The darkened valley spread.
  Hush ! God has said
His sunset word of love.

A MEMORY

TWO little hills,— my mountains then,—
   A small ravine between,
Beneath whose mystery of boughs
   The hollow heart of green
Was quick with tremulous fear, with hope
   Of fairer flowers unseen.

With childhood's wonder, innocent
   Of wiser scorn,
Plunging through rustling boughs back-bent,
   Moist with the morn,
Into the sprayed fantastic brake
   And crisp thin grass
Stirred with the swing of some swift snake, —
   To part and pass
The caverns of the gold and green
   Strange solitude
With fearful hopes of things unseen,
   Not surely good, —
To pluck the white stars, softly tinged
   With sunset skies
As cheeks in slumber — faintly fringed
   By half-shut eyes —
All this that was, the sense of bliss
   Unknowing, free,

PRÆTERITA

Quick with the wind, the sunshine's kiss,
  The smiling sea, —
All this has passed. New days have come,
  The book lies sealed.
The shrines are darkened, all is dumb,
  No word revealed.
Only, to-day, in hours that are
  Outworn with care,
Old memories brighten, break the bar,
  Once more are fair.
Once more — a moment — as life was,
  And then, but this,
As on the lips of them that pass
  Lies love's last kiss.

PRÆTERITA

THE world has quite outgrown her song,
  Because the world has sung too long,
And so the world shall sing no more,
And song is o'er.

For men are wiser than of old,
And men have learned the worth of gold,
And men have set their hearts above
The spell of love.

Men's eyes shall cease to weep, they say,
For pity, in the coming day,
And none shall laugh through all the earth
Made bare of mirth.

Then heaven that we hoped shall be
As the old tale of Arcady,
And men, in spirit as in breath,
Shall die in death.

The world has quite outgrown her song,
Because the world has sung too long,
And so the world shall sing no more,
And song is o'er.

THERE IS A MUSIC IN THE MARCH OF STARS.

THERE is a music in the march of stars,
  And song that fills the pulses of the sea,
  That whispers in the wind, and piteously
Sobs in the rain, a chant that grates and jars
In the dull thunder's heart, that makes or mars
  The song of nature, the world-song that we
  Hear loud above us, the great symphony
That throbs from life against death's barrier
    bars.

THE DAY IS DONE

What is the music of the song of life ?
  What is its theme, — of heaven or of hell ?
We know not : joy and grief and love and
    strife
Are mingled there, nor shall the answer be
  Till the great trumpet of God's doom
    shall tell
The thundered keynote to the land and sea.

THE DAY IS DONE

A BAR of cloud in the flaming west, —
  *The wind from the west, the wind
from the sun,*
And the black sea foaming from crest to
    crest,
  The day is done. The day is done.

Make sail upon the swaying mast,
  Into the night to meet the sun.
Sail ! for the darkness gathers fast,
  And the day is done. The day is done.

Leave hope behind, with her that is dead.
  Into the dark, Farewell, O sun!
Forget her eyes and her golden head.
  The day is done. The day is done.

SONGS OF EXILE

God of the sad, guide thou my feet,
*The wind blows red from the sinking
sun,*
When shall my heart forget my sweet ?
Now the day is done, now the day is done.

" Thou shalt sail the swaying world of sea,
And breast the rising of the sun,
But the grief of her eyes shall follow thee,
*Though the day is done, though the day
is done.*

" Thou shalt wander wide from place to
place.
Ah, God, the risings of the sun!
And everywhere thou shalt see her face."
*Ah, God, ah, God, were the day but
done!*

Away, away, up the ridging sea,
*What help in the sea, what help in
the sun ?*
Perhaps in death she will come to thee —
*When the day is done, when the day is
done.*

THE FIRST EDITION OF THIS BOOK CONSISTS
OF FIVE HUNDRED COPIES WITH THIRTY-
FIVE ADDITIONAL COPIES ON HAND—MADE
PAPER PRINTED DURING OCTOBER 1896 BY THE
ROCKWELL AND CHURCHILL PRESS OF BOSTON

www.ingramcontent.com/pod-product-compliance
Lightning Source LLC
Chambersburg PA
CBHW022152020726
47496CB00008B/2673